Nunzia Eleuteri

# The Human Capital Era

eBook edition only

AD✕GIO

www.adagioebook.it

*To my Family,*
*Past and Present*
*To all that's precious*
*and cannot be measured*

# Sommario

# INTRODUCTION

Accustomed to numbers, accustomed to budgets, accustomed to the world of economics and finance, I prefer that feeling that seems detached from all this and that is proper of the emotions world. Thus, after a decade spent working in a bank and a degree in banking and finance, I am writing today for passion as well as for work. Writing is therapeutic. Not only you discover what you have inside, but you also have an interlocutor of all respect: yourself. In addition to the alphabet and grammar rules, they should teach us, from an early age, that writing is an "output", a language for an external device of our hardware that puts us in a position to make effective and efficient our human "software". This "evolved" language also used by "machines" may seem inappropriate to a reading like this, but if it is the only one that today is required in order to keep up with the times, the only one mythicized by young people, the only one comprehensible by the finance systems, the only one that business owners consider infallible, I want to use it to communicate the only thing really worth focusing on: a human being is a machine, a perfect machine with a simulated gearing but with feelings and ways of doing unrepeatable. The human being, every man, is unique. Therefore, irreplaceable. We could also clone it: you would never have a perfect copy. It's a good of great value for its various specifics and for the life experiences that forges and that make it what it is. In the business world, it is often considered equal or even less important compared to the other tools and for this outclassed. However, it represents a material and immaterial good to which all realities, in business or not, should recognize a very different value. More or less high, more or less positive, the human being is a capital for every company, for every association. In this historical moment, unfortunately, we're losing sight of the human aspect and its complexity privileging soulless aspects such as machines and numbers (from personal data to wages and budgets). Just think about the selection of staff, a vital moment and one of the most important in a business setting. 70% is based on algorithms, without having CV's in front of the eyes of a human being. In the business world, automatic assumptions are increasing, where they are assigned to a program and to a machine. But what about the human being, does a man have a value? History is marked by various eras, each with strengths and weaknesses, in which a man was the star and creator but also a passive spectator. In any case, there. History is a succession of moments that have seen a man conscious of his power in the period of the Renaissance, blinded by the forms in the Baroque period and then he leaves the appearance and follows the reason in the Enlightenment period reaching the creativity and emotions of Romanticism. History has seen him return to scientific methods and objectivity of Naturalism and marry the "truth" in a Realism, often exasperated, flowing into the Decadent, with the acceptance of irrationality. In short, a continuous race, in search of himself, of happiness, of the best way to live. The Impressionism enhances what a man has in front while Expressionism wants to show the intimacy, what's on the inside. And then, here is Futurism. Here is the historical avant-garde that rejects the traditions and enhances the technology, the undisputed model of a capitalist society. And so the human limits generate anguish, that kind of mood related to existentialism, the search for answers about human existence. Is there a God? And here we are. The history continues. The questions remain unanswered. The mysteries remain undisclosed. Mankind  is always in frantic search of wellness. A well-being that made him slave of the superfluous and of which he cannot do without, transforming the surplus in necessity. That well-being is at the center of existence and generates an unstoppable vortex that involves every aspect of life and that is the engine of the economy: a subject that seems to scare everyone and that so many fill their mouths with giving the impression of having to do with some kind of science. The economy is however something very basic because it is born from the search of every individual to satisfy a need according to his preferences, and choosing, rationally, the optimal solutions for the achievement of its purpose. From here originates the market, the meeting of supply and demand in pursuit of the objectives of the parties involved: the maximum utility for the consumer and the maximum profit for the manufacturer. A trivial concept, of course, but from here I need to start giving voice to Domenico. A successful manager but first of all a human being. Meeting him was a little like meeting myself and the many other friends who have lived the same story and with whom, in the last years, I had the chance to stop and reflect. Several living rooms, telephones, virtual squares but the same subject: the meaning of life in a constant race. Today we are always running and twenty-four hours are not enough for a working day. We run even if we manage to have a minimum of free time and maybe even when we are sleeping! But for what? Which are the needs to satisfy? The rewards have become increasingly rare. The State has overwhelmed workers with harassment, relegating them to slavery. Employers convey to employees their dissatisfactions asking for higher performances and these, in order to maintain their positions, somersaults to please their superiors  and so on in an endless chain of human research for that sense of fulfillment that has become unreachable. Something does not work. We run as if we were at the last stretch of the race but someone constantly moves the finish line. So the energy sooner or later, will end. Or at least life will end without having lived it as we wished. And this is not enough. What is most disheartening is that you trample on feelings, moods and needs. A man is downtrodden just to reach destinations that change from time to time. No matter how good, honest, helpful you are and how much you have dedicated to a company, to politics, to an association. They pass on top of everything just to follow numbers, losing sight of the fact that, alone, they do not count. Numbers without a value are simply signs. And the story of Domenico is the litmus test!

This is the story of many managers that I've listened to making a synthesis. I told the story making it mine. It was not as hard as I thought it would be, because when there's empathy, one look is enough to understand each other. If the experience of those who are standing in front of you is similar to yours, then you even have the feeling of completing a puzzle. A right sense of observation is enough and... you magically find the pieces in your hands. The story, deliberately short to marry the needs of this time in which we are all constantly running, presents some assessments, taken from economists, a drop in the social reality in an alternation of emotions and practicality. The ambition, difficult I know, is to keep up hope that this society will reflect deeply on a theme that has become inescapable: what is man's value?

## THAT THURSDAY...

Me and my smile, always inseparable. The radiance that makes me so affable reflects my being. I am so, at work and in life. A feature that in its naturalness turned convenient at the right time and in the most unexpected situations. With this smile I face every beginning of the working week as well as every beginning of my weekly rest. But not that Thursday, the 15th of October... not after meeting my sales manager.

I'm ready to leave Milan to go back home, like every weekend. Sitting between desks and screens still on, I listen to the words of who's sitting in front of me, words that were previously only suspected but which are now reality. The budget, as if it could speak, will soon invite us to leave our positions become too onerous due to our "seniority". "Headcount restructuring" is the new corporate mission. I get immediate confrontation: are we only organic material? Apparently, nothing more. In a moment, a film is projected in and from my memory:

15

it's my life. I see my wife and my children, I see my parents now in heaven, I see my colleagues, my friends, I see my car travelling thousands of kilometers every year, I see my desk, the projects I'm working on and those completed with success. I see... just blankness. Still in the midst of the energy with my 53 years still to celebrate, still useful to corporate strategies, I can not believe what's happening as if something is falling on top of me with the weight of a boulder.

I stop. I think. Of course, as a good manager, I know my role is more expensive than that of a young graduate novice. I know that numbers don't have a soul and are therefore, according to one school of thought, uncontested. But I also know that numbers are not generated by themselves. Behind every infinitesimal there is who produces it: a human being! If it's a question of technology, statistics, production, cost, revenue, profit, taxes, rebates... it doesn't matter, behind there is always a human. There is an idea, there is sacrifice, there is labor, there is study, there is a forecast, there is an estimate. Each issue arises from all this individually or, almost always, from a set of actions. I think deep down. I try to understand with the person that I'm sitting with if there may be any solutions to get out of what I believe is just a misunderstanding or a bad strategic assessment. We make our own observations. The new restructuring involves cutting down two area managers and five employees. That's how it seems. I think of my team, my best friend Lorenzo who is a sole income earner and will remain soon without a job. I feel dwarfing, I'm afraid of losing consciousness. The only words that come out is a call for attention to the sensitivities of colleagues still unaware of what is happening: - "I want to be the one to warn them" - I say to the director - "I want to make sure that they are told in the best way and with a glimmer of hope for the future". I just need to figure out the best way to do it. The emptiness in my stomach becomes a chasm that sweeps away everything: the memories of the past and the faith in the future, but not my smile, my inseparable lifetime companion. So, I leave the office, with a smile:

17

this time of resignation. I walk along the corridor already imagining that it will no longer be my daily path. Incredulous, I observe the desk. Mentally I organize the move. Almost mechanically my eyes turned toward the picture of my wife and our children. How much sorrow will they feel? Their projects to be implemented, the studies to be completed, their career path to be built in a world where we are just numbers, where young people are discarded for lack of experience and adults shelved for a piece of personal data. Numbers. Nothing more. Soulless. Incontestable numbers. That's what we are. All of us.

## A MONSTER THAT DEVOURS SLEEP

Sleeping in the dark is the most natural thing. But not when the darkness is inside you. In that case insomnia reigns supreme and it is not the bearer of good dreams, good memories or good hopes. You have the darkness inside and you see the bleak on the outside. A uniformity that makes you feel overwhelmed and with no way out. You remember as a child that a prayer was enough to fall asleep peacefully. Now you don't even know where to start... Yet, a guardian angel to entrust all, it's what you would need. I toss and turn in search of the peace that you want more than anything else, but that doesn't arrive. The day light arrives before, finding you totally unprepared.

In a hotel room that I had to endure for years, waiting for life to take me back to work closer to home, I get up trying to improve my appearance. I look like a different man with different features. Aged suddenly. I think inevitably to my "personal data". I see my few wrinkles

19

that I had never given any importance. I look in the mirror. Just like Vitangelo Moscarda I try to understand who am I. One, none, a hundred thousand. How many are we??? Those wrinkles... There are those who hide them with make-up, those with cosmetic surgery and those who try to stop them with all sorts of miracle creams. I gaze at them. I analyse them. I approach the mirror and I follow the little furrows with my finger. What are wrinkles? They are our life! They are the inevitable witness of what we have been through the many years we have lived.

How can my wrinkles be, not just two large grooves around the lips, that draw that smile that always accompanied me? Expression lines, that's all. And now in front of the mirror a smile comes back... It's a melancholy one, but it's back again. This new discovery gives me the urge to wash, dress nicer than ever and go back to the office. There are a thousand things to do, a thousand paths to try, many friends with whom to share this state of mind, to think about alternatives. And there is my family to inform. Yeah... my family. The anguish comes back together with the fear of not succeeding. The weariness of the sleepless night is displayed in all its power and it terrifies me again. I won't be able to go to the office. It's going to be a really terrible Friday. I wonder if it's true that evil spirits were created on Friday but what I certainly know is that this Friday has got nothing of positive. The memories start overlapping until going back to Canada where I was born and lived for a few years and where I wanted to go back, after graduation, leaving university, to go and learn English well and throw myself, impatient, in the labour market. I had so many projects in mind, so much vitality, so much hope. Today no project, a heavy heart and zero prospects. I suddenly feel naked. I feel like that November the 10th, 1969, when my mother died. That child was only six years old. Today, I have the feeling that, that's where I've stopped. If it were not for my personal data... I would still be convinced of being still that child. Mom, you left me again??? This is what my heart is silently screaming and this is the anger that wants to explode, aware of the fact that we always look

21

for the support and the clash of those that we love most in the world! With the big and bright eyes of a child I cry: "Mom, where are you?". A renewed sense of abandonment takes my breath away. I cry. I am a man with a piece of personal data so compromising that he cries. We don't cry very often. Still crying is the "greatness" that our body can not contain and that releases in the form of tears. Water and salt. Life and bitterness. A man cries throughout his maturity. This man, as I am, cries for a mom who would beg for a hug. If only for a moment. Nothing makes us feel safer than in the arms of our mother. Nothing is more comforting. Nothing is more welcoming. Mom. We all need it. At any age. An inseparable and irreplaceable bond. A bond that evolves over time and that, while aging, remains strong and vital. I cry, I cry for a mother who is no longer here. A mom that I have known little but I loved so much, imagining her always by my side: at school, with friends, at my wedding, when I became a father. I always pictured her next to me. Perhaps it's for this reason that my smile accompanied me for a lifetime.

# I LOOK BACK

I believe that there is nothing that can complete a feeling of loneliness like a hotel room. Perhaps a spaceship. That one yes! In a cold city, amid the indifference of millions of people, away from those you love, yes, nothing can compete with a hotel room to empty even more a body and a mind already empty.

I lie on the bed, still without strength or ideas to address this Friday that will take me back to my family as usual, as it has been happening for more than ten years. I turn on the computer hoping that my soul illuminates. I look for something to cling on, and, as often happens, who seeks finds. Among the many phrases that appear on the socials, one is in the foreground, in front of my eyes: "Nothing will prevent the sun to rise again, not even the darkest night. Because beyond the black curtain of night there is a dawn that awaits us". The author is Khalil Gibran. Nothing could be more suitable for the day. The

23

thoughts continue to overlap between memories and intentions. One of them makes me smile bitterly. It's been a while that I've been wanting to go back home without having to leave my wife alone anymore during the week. I wanted to greet her in the morning, after a good coffee together, and sleep at night by her side. The children, now grown up, are at University, leaving a huge void in the house that a woman more than a man can not bear even though she doesn't get bored certainly with her rather demanding and prestigious job. It was our goal in life that I would return as soon as possible closer to home. A legitimate life objective but a goal not easy when you have a responsible position like mine in a multinational company. What a strange life! Before you run all the time trying to realize a professional dream, obtain economic tranquillity and that well-being that will let you afford to raise your children and give them a home and a perspective of study and work. Then during the race you realize that you have succeeded, that you have crossed the finish line several times without even catching your breath.

24

You kept running: you were trained. If we look in the mirror we would see a hamster on a wheel, I know... But that wheel can not stop because it produces, because it makes you feel good, because it keeps you active, it keeps your standard of living, your home, your children and their projects. You're on a wheel yet you feel on a swing: sometimes slave and sometimes master of your life. I arrived at 53 years of age, with two children about to graduate, I had definitely planned to steer that wheel towards home, but continuing to run... And now, I smile, in a derisive way, life has accomplished me fulfilling my project. I'm going back home, maybe. But not as I wanted. Nor how my Edda pictured it. I think back to ten years ago when I found myself changing job after eighteen years and starting a new one in another large multinational company. It was not easy but the mood was different: I was going to make a leap forward. An upgraded career. I sought an agreement with the personnel department that suited both, I felt butterflies in my stomach, butterflies of one who jumps on a trampoline. But the jump, that time, had

25

been prepared and I knew that the landing was going to be comfortable. But now the jump was like stepping into the dark. I do not know the height, I do not know the ground, I do not know if I'm sufficiently athletic to do it but I have no choice. They will push me and I can only try to do my best to save at least the bones. I think back to my colleagues who greeted me and how I greeted them. Among all I recall Gianluca, Marcello, Vittorio and Mariolina. "Area Managers" just like me, and today with their different professional careers and lives. We maintained a good relationship: phone calls, dinners. The affection is not ended by changing a job or with a contract. We are men before colleagues. There are feelings and there is esteem. Then I stop. A sudden light illuminated me: Mariolina. Only a few months ago I asked her as a joke to get me to work with her. A choice that would have lead me home, at last. It was July, we were having dinner together, one of the many dinners organized with friends. She replied, "Maybe! But you are going to cost us too much" I replied that money is not everything in life. It remained only a joke that made us smile. I will call Mariolina.

## IN MY CAR

My car... If it had a soul it would be my best friend. The one with whom I spent more time, the one that knows my deepest anxieties, my worries, the one that knows my discussions over the phone, my plans, my dreams, my favourite music. But it is a machine and the limits of all machines is that they are not a human being! It's just a tool that humans can use. Like the computer, the phone... Tools. A big difference compared to us my dear "head count restructuring". A car without a good pilot doesn't move or it can even crash somewhere.

The mind always returns there: to yesterday's unexpected communication. Thursday, October 15th. I collect ideas. I will not go to the office this morning. I will move up my return home. I sit in the car and I leave. I can not wait to talk to my Edda and find with her a bit of serenity. And I want to spend a weekend without thinking about anything. I want to go for a walk and take her back to my home where I grew up with my father

29

and my brother, I want to breathe the fresh air that makes me feel at home. Only that air can bring me back in time as if it had never passed. I want to taste all that this beautiful life offers us and that we cannot contemplate on the hamster wheel. Here's what I want! "I willed, I willed and very strongly I willed"! I smile thinking back to my diploma in accounting and my Italian teacher. He would be happy to hear that I have some memory of literature. Many think that in a technical institute some subjects are not explored deeply. But everything, as always, depends on the people not on the containers in which they operate. It depends on who gives and who receives, it's the people that make the difference. In every field. In every company. In every school. Always a man with his characteristics. Too bad that "my" beautiful multinational didn't understand it. At school I was lucky. Was it luck or was it all planned? Or everything worked better than today? Or are the values of the past more solid? The fact is that I had very good Professors, the very rare ones to find. Those who know how to make you passionate about life even before making you passionate about books. Of course, as always, we appreciate them later... And so, very often, I find myself quoting poets and authors in the reports of my financial statements. It's true that sooner or later you put to good use all the acquired assets. And then you discover that nothing of what you have done is useless. Everything is part of that journey that began the day of your birth. And nothing is left to chance. Pain, joys, sacrifices and satisfactions are the routes that you can take to learn about the city of your life and enjoy it in full. You can not see the beautiful view that the tower offers if you don't go up all the stairs, even the most steep and uneven ones, stumbling and standing up again. These are things that I know, that I always thought, that made me what I am, bright and positive. Always. I'm that guy (this is how I still feel! No matter what the heavy piece of personal data for the headcount says !!!) I am the guy who greets people looking straight in the eyes, that smiles, that gives himself away whenever needed. This is the way I am. They taught me to be so. Those little

31

rules of good manners that make better coexistence in every context and that should be taught at school to be sure to fill in the gaps of some families. If in school, they also taught the manners of good society... If they had the foresight to understand that it is an out dated text, but more modern than ever, which is not only about the form but about the substance, which is not only affectation but it's respect, I believe that social relations would realize an inestimable benefit. Basic education, starting from mutual respect and friendliness, allowed me to grow professionally as well as humanly. My clients, my suppliers, my colleagues and my friends appreciate me for who I am whether at work before a contract of millions of euro or in a bar enjoying some carefree moments. I like the relationship, the human relationship. Just talk to me once and you will understand it immediately. Finding myself at the table with friends is one of the things that I prefer, and I often do it because I think loneliness is the worst of evils. It takes away all your powers making you not only helpless but unaware of the skills you have. It takes you by the throat, suffocating you, taking away all your energy and even fading your voice. You are alone: why would you want to talk? Solitude. A monster like insomnia. Absolutely to fight! Sharing is one of my rules of life. Relationships and sharing. I like it and I want to continue like this. And the first with whom I share everything are those who I love the most: my wife and my children. I get ready to see them.

## My family

The biggest thought is of my family: what can I say, how can I tell them, to whom shall I say it before and to whom not? A thousand thoughts and fears assail me... I'll talk to my Edda. She will help me to do the other steps and decide together how to tell our children.

I try to prepare a speech during the drive. I imagine a thousand different beginnings. Once arrived at destination, I find myself to be as positive as ever. I look at my love in the eyes and I say: - "Edda I have good news for you! I'm coming back home!". Lately, with her typical way of an intelligent woman, she has been making it clear to me, that she would rather have me closer to her. We sit down. I start telling her the story of the last few hours of my life. We deepen, then finally, she emits one of the most beautiful and reassuring sounds I've ever heard: - "Don't worry, you will choose your next job". When a woman is able to amaze you after decades of relationship it means that you have in front of you a special woman. I do not know how many would have responded well to a story like that. I do not know, but for me it was enough to confirm that I was lucky to have met her and that we had given life to our family together! After this first step, another one to make: talk to the children. How shall we say it to our children?

There is always this primordial instinct to want to protect our children from any regrets, any pain, even in the knowledge that the forge pain, strengthens, stimulates the reaction. In short, pain makes you grow. How can a child learn to be strong enough to stand up if you never let him fall? I remember a famous psychologist who, one evening, a few months ago, in front of a large audience, testified that the biggest problem of the young patients that he had in his care, was that they all suffered from a low self-esteem. Many suicides of young people appear linked to their inability to react to pain, to a refusal, at a minimum dissatisfaction. "They are not used to." He said. They are no longer accustomed to suffering, to receive a "no" as an answer. He had asked those present if they had seen children with scars on their knees. He immediately replied that they don't exist anymore. Children no longer fall off their bikes because parents are above them with bated breath to avoid the slightest painful approach. "And so" - he said - "children may not know that they have the strength to get up again because they have never fallen". Mindful of this speech that had intrigued me, even though I felt a different parent, I can do the simplest thing: put my children in front of reality. They are old enough to deal with it and it will also be a useful experience for them in life. My older son, Francesco, didn't surprise me, his reaction shows me that he's a mature and sensitive guy. After a first short moment of disbelief, follows his statement: - "These things happen, now we must think about how to move". After the many fears that had accompanied me, his words gave me greater confidence and the certainty of having a wonderful family and a grown up son. His sister Elena, my younger daughter, I must admit causes me a bit more anxiety. I can not tell her; maybe she is not as ready or maybe I'm the one not ready? The fact of not having the certainty of a safe job raises the problem of revising some economic aspects such as support to complete university courses for my children. This gives me a strange feeling of guilt even though I know that I can not blame myself for something that does not depend on me. We ask our Elena, close to her three-year degree, what does she think about the opportunity of attending the master degree in our city instead of Florence. She already understood everything! My women are, to say the least, surprising! Now I just have to tell my brother. I decide to wait. I do not want him to worry. When the picture of the situation will be clearer, I'll call him.

## HOME EQUALS LOVE

There is nothing more comforting than being at home. Embracing a beautiful wife that you have loved for years and with whom you share everything. Weakness? I think love is something quite different: a hundredfold strength!

Edda and me. Over a quarter of a century together. An evolution of feelings, so different but so chained up to be indissoluble. From a first phase of falling in love to a stronger and concrete one, through moments of reflection, maybe even second thoughts and yes ,crisis, followed by a mature and solid love, made of mistakes, falls, of willpower, emotions, I think this is the most beautiful married life experience that you can tell. And we can do it! How many things we have faced and overcome! We are going to make it even this time! After a dogs Thursday, I'm living a lions Friday. I do not know why but now I have a strange feeling of positivity in me. It's just like going back to when you were a child and you do something for the first time: you feel the adrenaline rising as you face the unknown... I do not know how to explain it. Is it a natural self-defence mechanism of the mind or is it a strong optimism? What I know is that I am smiling next to my wife, I have two wonderful children and I have the strength to face the difficulties, I am hundreds of kilometres away from the place where I work and I'm getting ready to see my friends for dinner.

## MEETINGS

The evening at the restaurant passes pleasantly. I had no doubts despite the fact that I felt on me all the tiredness of the terrible night I had spent.

During the dinner we talked about many stories. There was laughter, but we also talked about serious things, unfortunately unavoidable, seeing the historical moment that we are living. We would need important and vital reforms but they are unattainable considering the fact that we have the worst political class of all time. The Right, the Left... Once we used to discuss of proposals and ideas, of opposing values. Today there is no distinction. It's a popular banality to say that they are all the same but this is it! The political world is leaning towards an individualism that does not leave space for the interest of the collective well-being now outclassed by the demon "money." A policy that can not answer to people. A policy that cannot give hope to the young ones, abandoning them to high unemployment rates. A policy that does not know how to protect the old ones relegating them to the company's corners with starvation pensions. It cannot even guarantee me that I am in the limbo! It considers me too old to work, facilitates the company to send me to "rest" but considers me too young for a decent pension. The political and labor world are parallel tracks that seem not to touch each other anymore. However, they are still going in the same direction: abyss. If you do not give the right value to a man, if you do not recognize its centrality compared to everything else, to every budget, to every strategy, every project, this civil society will be doomed to the abyss. Nothing more.

So between protests and smiles the evening comes to an end. We say goodbye with a commitment to see each other soon. A pleasant effort. I see, among others, Mariolina that I had spoken with on the phone a few hours earlier, telling her that I wanted to talk to her. We spent many years together in the multinational company where I worked until ten years ago. She told me, last July, that she was in a transitional phase. The multinational was selling a line of business, and she was going to be the sales director. A career in advancement. How beautiful!!! I had congratulated her with all the naturalness in my heart and that always makes me share the joys of others rather than the pains. It's easier to feel close to others in compassion rather than in a glorification of a success. Instead, I am always happy about the good things as if they are happening to me. At that dinner in July, we agreed that I would help her build her team. During the last months, I have sent her different curriculum of the young account managers that I had the chance to get to know and appreciate and that they all had the right credentials to do well. It's a role much sought today by companies and where the "gap" between supply and demand is very big. It seems that dealing with sales is not a very coveted job. Just a few young people are open to do so but with the claim of an immediate final job contract without understanding that this is the worst business card they can present to any company. Selling was my world. It helped me to go around Italy and many other countries, to get to know many people and grow professionally and personally. It gave me economic and personal gratification but what I liked the most was the human contact, a basic element and keystone of this area. Often young people have fear or are even ashamed to deal with the commercial area of a company. There is no shame in any job if you do it with honesty and transparency. The secret, if this is what we are talking about, of a good sale, is not in the manuals to be purchased in bookstores, all the same... It is not even in the training courses or master's degrees. It is in the way of being and attitude. Friendliness and listening skills are, for example, two of the basic elements that should be part of the cultural background of everybody, that baggage I was talking about earlier: education and respect. If you listen to the customer, you understand what his or her needs are; so you can find the best solutions. Not the most expensive one that can bring more profit but the best one! This is called intellectual honesty and is another cardinal principle needed in a good business. The best offer for the customer, of a quality product, is, of course, the one that will make him so happy to never have the need to change suppliers. If the best deal also involves friendliness, the working relationship can only continue in loyalty. There might be problems, stumbles, complications but if there is underlying friendliness, quality, professionalism and honesty, everything is surmountable. There is no need for sales manuals... So, I sent Mariolina the resumes of those candidates who I thought had all the necessary features to take the path that I had started twenty-eight years ago with an increasing of responsibility and rewards. Just like her.

One of them, to my great satisfaction, is currently working in northern Italy as area manager. I hardly go wrong in evaluating a guy, because I do it with great objectivity. Judgment is not for mortifying but is to find a talent. That's what we all have but we often do not know how to recognize it. Very good are those Professors who apply this principle in schools... A principle that strengthens and does not demotivate. In short, after proposing to Mariolina candidates to form her team, I find myself to be the one of them. I tell her that my company seems to want to proceed with staff restructuring and that inevitably will invest in my role and that of other colleagues. We speak of the possibility of me becoming part of her team, this time it's not a joke as it was in July. She looks at me and she says: - "Maybe Domenico! I do not have a suitable job for you at your current contract level but we can provide a role as a key account manager. You are worth more and we both know it. Your experience, reliability, dedication and your way of being, do not have equals for me! You are a guarantee! I would be delighted to have you at my side. If that's okay, we can speak as soon as possible to understand how we can proceed". I turned to stone. I had requested an interview, yes, but I never thought to have such a quick response. She has been so concrete, leaving me speechless. I should have known... typical of intelligent women. In a moment they are able to find many different solutions, maybe this is their innate gift due to the spirit of survival that, over the centuries, saw them giving birth to many children. Always accustomed to thinking about others and not for themselves, women can be multifunctional. For this, the intelligent ones are kept away from powerful positions. I think it's jealousy. I would never have imagined that just a few hours after learning that I may have lost my job, I would have been able to find another. Life is strange. Made of people and miracles that too often we do not even know how to recognize: meetings.

## A RESTFUL SLEEP

Sometimes it seems that life is already written, and you're just a mannequin. Meetings and coincidences that you cannot consider as they are, put you in a state of disbelief. You think, inevitably that the guardian angel that you don't know how to find anymore and to whom you entrust all your anxieties, is however there always by your side driving your car in the right direction. The one that you don't even know anything about. But he does...

I go back home. That unexplainable feeling of positivity, now finds an explanation: a new life prospective. I will have a lower salary but I do not care. I'm happy for one thing above all: the person that I am, and that put me in a position to find a new job in a few hours thanks to a colleague's esteem. I'm glad of the reasons that Mariolina has given me, I feel gratified by what I have sown over the years: a dispassionate and sincere friendship that puts me now in a privilege situation. Those values of honesty, reliability, respect, positivity have awarded me, regardless of my personal data. Values that I have passed on, with full commitment, to my children: values that have got no age! The same that I found in Mariolina who knew how to recognize and appreciate them, humanizing that piece of personal data and that accounting data reported in the payroll at the end of the month. Those numbers should have a soul and should be the result of what we are. Mariolina left me saying that she would think on how to proceed. I am beset by the doubt that the multinational that I had left ten years earlier will have no intention of having me back. Even if for a short time considering the impending sale of the business unit. I wonder if Mariolina had thought about this hypothesis. I lie in bed, next to my wife. We retrace together all these last 36 intense hours of life. She struck me with her reassuring voice: "Don't worry Domenico, Mariolina knows your qualities. I told you that you were going to choose your next job. You wait and see, this is what will happen." Now I feel calmer and I finally collapse into a deep and restful sleep.

## AN ORDINARY SATURDAY

The saying "sleep on it" is a timeless advice. The clarity that you have after resting the mind is really impressive. If after a good rest you combine a pleasant distraction, they gather forces that seemed lost forever. Sometimes, this alone could be enough to prevent a suicide. It's a shame that you can not be close to those who feel so alone...

I seem to have slept for days. I open my eyes and I struggle a bit to understand where I am and that all what had happened was not just a bad dream. It's that sense of disorientation of someone who is used to sleeping away from home frequently. Before getting out of bed, you have to focus on the wall that you have in front of you and realize where exactly did your body find rest. In a few hours I went from feeling a sense of abandonment and emptiness to a feeling of vitality and fullness. Now I do not know which of the two sensations will accompany me through this day: the possibility of not having my job anymore or the hope that soon I will have a new one? I just know that I have a primordial need to be fulfilled: to breathe the air of my childhood. Visit the graves of my father and my mother. I want to tell my father that he was right: I should not have left the corporation where I had worked for eighteen years and chosen the one that today does not hesitate to do without me. My father did not appreciate that choice. He did not like this company... But as you know, children never follow the advices of their parents. As too often happens, they eventually find themselves, like me, admitting that they should had listen to those recommendations. Life is a wheel. Yesterday I was a child, today I am a father. And the perspective is turned upside down in an instant. I get in the car, with my wife, as in an ordinary Saturday and we reach our "blue mountains" of Giacomo Leopardi where it is not hard to find yourself, nor rare to find yourself seeking for the Infinite and feeling part of it. I think of the many, too many, religion wars linked to a different God's name that human beings have always sought. But what can it mean a name when you are talking about interiority and immensity? How can a man kill another man just for a name? Only the inability to recognize the very small and insignificant dimension that makes so much damage and cause so much pain! How much stupidity in men! After all, what can we expect if even in the place where we work is not uncommon to find someone ready to hurt you for nothing? Indeed, not for nothing but for envy, for the peculiarities of those who throughout their life try to trudge brooding jealousies and grudges, wishing misfortune to those who are better than them. I can not even imagine how they manage to live like this! Envy is an acid that eats you and ends up making you sick. Yet there are those who cannot do without feeding it more and more. Sometimes exacerbating it until death... if only those energies were destined to find the qualities in themselves and in others, there would be room for everyone. I have a dear friend, a sociologist, who is presently devoting his time to prove that there is no intelligence, but there are a multiple of intelligences. Intelligences ranging between many skills and knowledge. In the envious, however, stupidity wins. Rather than use what they have and what they know, they waste their time with bitterness and jealousy. How many I have met along my way! Conceited that never question themselves, thinking they know everything or assume they are suitable for any role. And if these behaviours are seasoned with envy and malice, the union is one of the worst kind. However, all the chickens come home to roost and I have often experienced situations where I could have rejoiced with "I told you so" but I remained silent. It is not my style. Although they do not enjoy my esteem, the opinionated and the arrogant have never seen me celebrating their failures. Maybe because I feel sorry for them. Maybe because I know that we can all make mistakes and I always like to give a second chance, even to those who do not deserve it. A mistake, in my way of being, is conceived as an opportunity: to correct ourselves. Unfortunately not many understand and persevere. Others, however, completely change as if they are living a second birth. If we think deeper, it is a concept of re-education of the wicked. Another twisted argument, in a world that seeks punishment at all costs as a satisfaction after experiencing a painful injustice, rather than a recovery for those who have made a mistake more or less severe. If I think about it, the idea that the world still has a death penalty and retaliation law makes me shudder. I love to give everyone a second chance, to be honest I often grant a third or a fourth one... And there is someone that says that I'm too good, on the border of stupidity. But this is the way I am.

Hand in hand, me and Edda go through the alleys of our homeland up in the mountain. We sniff, as hounds, the smells that take us back in time. We greet the many familiar faces that we meet and that make us feel part of a big family. This is the beauty of small communities. In cities you lose the identity, you are nobody, a resident like so many, a number. Just as in large companies. The small villages give you a name, often more than one. It gives you consideration, for better or for worse. It embraces you between dynamics of gossip and stories, between the authenticity of its products, including memories of those who were there and are now no longer with us, including the faces of children who you recognize only because they look like their parents that used to play with you. The countryside gives you the real feeling of being at home. Roots. That's all. And of this I was thirsty and hungry as a refugee who fasts for days away from his land.

## A DIFFERENT MONDAY

The "Monday syndrome" seems to have become such a common illness that you can find lots of explanations in many psychology scripts. It's the resumption of routine, you leave that wonderful free time to dive back into work issues. It's the effort of waiting for another weekend. Tuesday is already better, you are already inside what you were afraid of and you've already figured out that you can make it. In fact you can make it and another Friday will arrive, making you feel euphoric thinking of two days of relaxation. Then the wheels turn again and the weeks pass, even the months, then the seasons and the years go flying by. And then that Monday comes back undaunted still with a double weight compared to the other days...

My discomfort is not a syndrome. Not this time. This beginning of the week is not like the others. Together with the thousands of commitments already scheduled on the agenda, there is the meeting with my team to make them aware of these changes. Inevitably it makes me anguish. I am a human being, not only a manager. And this man knows his collaborators, knows their plans, knows their fears, their strengths, their weaknesses, their favourite football team referred to in the early hours of every Monday. He knows the looks of disappointment like those of joy. Work is not divorced from life. It is part of it. Sometimes too much! Working together is also sharing a mood that goes beyond that environment and that embraces the homes and families of all. Any problems or personal successes spill over others.

We are human beings, yes! If we are happy, we work hard, if we are sad we go a bit more slowly. "We are not machines!!! WE ARE HUMAN BEINGS!!!". I cry with all the breath in my throat as I drive my Faraday box to my office. I cry to relieve all the anxiety accumulated, I cry in protest. I cry for relief, I cry for defence, I cry for acceptance. I cry in the car and my eyes go bright again. I think of Andrea and that these days he was planning to treat his wife to  a trip for their first

Christmas together. Every morning, in front of a coffee, he was asking us if it was better the sea or the mountains, the cities of art or a relaxing spa. Each of us, with a real interest, pulled out of the hat the proposal of the century. Carlo for days kept arriving in the office with at least three car magazines. He absolutely has to buy one. He can not "steal" one from the parents and leave them each morning fighting for the other one. And there is Pina. Pina has been dreaming for almost a year to be able to tell her husband that they will finally expect the child they were waiting for. She is concerned about the work and she doesn't want to create too much discomfort during her brief period of maternity. I think of all of them. They will be upset. This Monday has nothing to do with the others. I will have the task of sweeping away the dreams of these kids. I will have to tell Andrea that it is better to postpone the Christmas trip, Carlo to wait before buying the car that will finally make him independent and I have to tell Pina not to hurry to have a baby... I can also see the others. We are twenty. A real premiership football team, but this time there will be nobody on the benches or in the stands... Someone will watch their team-mates play from home. Not only me, not only Lorenzo, my friend and colleague for life but also the others. My team will be blown away by this restructuring, on which I have a lot to say. I arrive at destination. I gather all the strength that I have and I reach the elevator. How strange, you do the same path for years and you only now notice details that you've never seen before, doors that suddenly seem to have materialized or walls that seemed to have a different colour... Who says that the gaze does not have a soul is wrong. This morning everything seems to be different and yet I have been here for exactly ten years. I enter the office and I find them all at their seats. I have a lump in my throat and I realize that I cannot speak. I decide to postpone the discussion to a later date. One thing that does not belong to me is to postpone, I would rather face it immediately. But this time, in fact, everything looks different. Me too.

## THAT STRANGE FEELING OF LOSING SOMETHING

Going to work without a perspective is the worst way of getting out of bed every morning. I do not know how those people that don't even like their jobs can handle it. It would be like going every day towards a conviction. Spending most of the time without a big motivation must be very mortifying. And if the only motivation is the salary then that's when you are trapped.

These days I feel like a robot without professional dignity. In the last twenty years of life, I used to think of myself and see myself as the others used to see me: a capable and successful manager (with the limits of my role, of course, but this is how it was). In the end, everything is relative in the world. At fifty years of age you feel young among the old and you feel old among the teenagers. Relativity is a concept that everyone should keep in mind. Who feels immensely powerful should think that they are only hung on a huge spinning ball suspended in the Universe. Notwithstanding this principle, in my world, Domenico was considered "great" and that's how I saw myself too within the work context. I have the undisputed relational skills, professionalism, knowledge, determination and concreteness that always lead me to achieve business goals. Now, suddenly, the meltdown. I feel a nobody.

How can it be possible that, out of the blue, someone had thought that I wasn't worth enough to keep me or even validate myself even more? Annihilated. Here's how I feel. All right, I tell myself that no one is indispensable, yet I see my uniqueness and irreplaceability. I didn't feel as a number among many others. At least not until that damned Thursday. My professional dignity is gone, along with my many years of work and my many expectations. Yes, despite my piece of personal data, I admit, I kept dreaming. Who stops dreaming, stops living. I'll dream as long as I can. I will keep dreaming until I am a hundred years old if life will allow me so much! Between hope and discussions, days have passed. I heard from Mariolina and the chance to get back with her in the company where I worked for eighteen years was getting real. At this point I am not worried for me anymore. I realized that, somehow, my skills will be put to the service of someone and, as my wife says, I can choose to accept or not. This negativity that hardly leaves me is linked to the uncertainty of all my colleagues future but of one in particular, Lorenzo, who has really shared with me my professional life journey. We have been so close for years. We love each other as brothers and knowing that he will have to face many difficulties now that his wife doesn't have a job and all the responsibility of his family rests on his shoulders, I just cannot accept it! These mornings, I carry my legs towards what will no longer be my desk, although I keep doing the same things, I continue making appointments with customers, I continue to participate in meetings. I have already the feeling that I have lost something.

The state of mind with which I face the day is different and therefore different is also the way of living it. Yes I understand that what I'm missing is the routine. Routine is a "beast" that can even devour your joy but that can also often be like a soft blanket that makes you feel that warmth that only security can give. Comparable to a gilded cage. Here's what I lost. I'm going to meet the new and inevitably I'm going to meet the unknown. To start a new experience is as exciting as distressing. Despite my proven qualities and capabilities, strong is the fear of not succeeding. When there is fear you feel paralyzed: you would like to go on but you can not take another step. You look back knowing what you are leaving and you look ahead with trepidation. You would like to have the audacity of that boy that you no longer are. You would like to jump off that swing that is making you sick and you would like do it with a great jump, aware of the fact that you could smash your bones but anyway you don't care, you keep going. Instead, I am scared and for now I'm not going to jump. Here I am paralyzed. Just like this economy that no longer knows which way to go. I think of the many texts that I read and how many opposing arguments! Many different schools of thought come and go through the years. Each has its own point of view and when you value them, you do not know which one to choose because they all look good as useless at the same time. Because, today, the political economy of private entities does not go hand in hand with the public one and there isn't an appropriate monetary policy correspondence. For those like me, who know the labor market and so the efficiency at any cost, the slowness of institutions that too often have leaders not adequate to the role, using an euphemism, becomes unacceptable. To be harsh, however, I think that too often there are people who are true round number such as a zero! Yet they are there. Professionalism should be "sine qua non" in all sectors but the truth is that, too often, those who are unsuitable for a role can obtain unconditional trust only from a kind of political privilege that almost hides mysterious motivations. Not quite mysterious to tell the truth, just a fair friend in the right place. A sad "rule" that I also saw applied in businesses, schools, in offices, in associations and in sports. This century has already been marked by this. Meritocracy does not live

65

here, in our country, in which nobody knows how to rebel. Where there aren't many protests and the ones that we have are often politically driven. We have become a nation of sheep. Or resigned? I do not know. Yet I feel this blood boiling in the face of injustice, in theft, in front of dishonesty and individualism of who should represent us in Parliament or in the Government. I feel this movement of rebellion but I also see around me that everything is silent and doesn't move. Only a few complaints among friends sat at a table. We have also lost the spirit of fighting for what is right. So today is the day that I have the feeling of having lost something: from the routine to the desire to revolt. Even worse, though, is the feeling to let go everything as it is... I am resigned. This is not me.

## WHAT IS MAN'S VALUE?

A human being is the most important capital and despite this he's always put in the background. Entrepreneurs and managers are so focused on adopting new software, on buying innovative machines, on analysing financial statements, that they have forgotten to get to know their most important assets: their people! They talk about wages, cuts... But do they know what a wage is? Where does it start from, how do you established it and how and why it should evolve?

It's Monday, October 26th and it seems a century since that Thursday when I realized that the company was planning "structural changes for strategic requirements" on which I would have to write an encyclopedia to justify their wrong assessment. The days have passed in a strange way, with a fast slowness. A contraposition in terms, I know, but the most faithful representation of what it was. As far as I'm concerned, it's sad to say for me, I never put money first and I am left with only one interest: maximize the economic aspect of my exit from a company that wants to give up on my skills.

I see myself propelled towards the new experience on Mariolina's team, who is meanwhile, perfecting my return to where I used to work a decade ago. There are still some difficult times in which my stomach has to defend itself from the corrosive acid digestive juices that have unfortunately become my constant companions.

Many unpleasant situations started to emerge. Colleagues that lack sensitivity, managers who are surprised by the way I am, calling me a "special" person but then giving up on me to follow a numerical trend, a flurry of assessments that result simply in mere contradictions between words and deeds. I think that the main activity of any director or officer or manager in any industry should be to talk to the human resources with which they collaborate. To know them better in issues such as aspirations and make the most of the talents of each one. Just because they are resources, too often however, a monitor that projects data takes over everything. My experience seems the exact opposite of what you might read in so many textbooks. I wonder if I'm writing another page in economic history since the economy is recognized by Viner as "a science that can not be called a once and for all because it's in continuous development according to the historical moments". Yet, I am convinced that what economists have studied over the years should at least be a starting point. Isn't this the reason why we need history? Don't we need it to avoid the mistakes of the past and to build the future on those experiences? Clark, for example, argues that it is a natural law to regulate income distribution. A law according to which the income of each person should correspond to its contribution to production. How can they establish, then, my contribution if they don't know me enough to remain surprised by my way of being that has been the same for a lifetime?! I think, then, about the marginal productivity analysis according to which the company demands for work up to the point where the productivity of the last worker hired is equal to the salary that has been paid. Who are the directors or managers that determine who costs too much? And how? Do they have a real knowledge of the productive resources? A staff director, for example, should be like a parent: he should know his children in order to recognize when they are sleepy and  when they are hyperactive! Marshall argues that every business owner should make the most beneficial use of resources and to achieve the best result, he must apply the principle of substitution between the productive inputs. The question that a good entrepreneur and administrator should be able to answer is this: how and when the work of a man can be replaced by other factors, human or technological-instrumental?  The answer cannot be just a number in the budget but a broader assessment that knows how to go from a work environment to an external relationship with customers and suppliers, and so on. That's what economists have been able to focus on over the years, studying the difficult relationship between the labor market's supply and demand in which we are all bargaining chips. They have been able to identify even a right "family economy".  Considering the workers as persons that don't generally live alone and that they have to make decisions depending also on their family, establishing the place where to live, whether to have children and how much to invest for them, if they have elder members to take care of, how and what to consume and how much to save, and so on. A man is a complex reality and can therefore give the best only if put in the position to do so. The job supply is strongly linked to all this. It can not be disregarded. The considerations that Lester wrote about in the '50s, that the most important ambitions of each worker are, of course, the economic security and the chance to improve their professional skills with a fair deal, but it's also the sense of belonging to a work community remains valid even today. To feel part of a big family can only push you to the utmost dedication. It's a feeling that I have always felt and I never thought that this family would put me at the door one day saying "we don't need you anymore". But I know that employment relationships are complex, so complex to provide a contract which, however, should be more like that of a

71

marriage rather than that of a consumer goods trading. Instead we stylize and generalize something so personal: the contract. The employee wants to receive fair treatment that goes from a fair wage, according to his performance, to the feeling of being part of a big family. On the other hand, the employer wants to get results from the commitment and wants professional capacity. A special combination between trust and mutual exchanges. Too often, however, there are not these elements at the base of the employment relationship. There are only and exclusively economic aspects. You search for the lowest labor cost, knowing that in a crisis, men adapt to everything debasing the skills acquired and "selling themselves" for a few dollars. This is exactly the famous Phillips curve, the economist that verified the inverse relationship between unemployment and wage trends. Layoffs for corporate restructuring are carried out in periods of crisis and unemployment. Periods in which wages are lowered because the supply of labor far exceeds demand by finding the meeting point at the bottom. But is it a true meeting point? The employer loses sight of the primary objective: what's best for his company, giving up on the high levels of professionalism and the worker loses his dignity just for little money. All this just to pursue one of the many aspects of the labor market: the economy. The God of money, in this era of individualism in which everything has a price and everything is for sale, dominates. But what is man's value? I think it's time for managerial humanism. You can no longer postpone. Modern economic literature writes a lot about human capital and speaks of "individual knowledge and skills as key elements that serve enterprises to respond adequately to the needs of an advanced economy". Schultz, Nobel Prize winner and University Professor in Chicago, in the recent 70's and 80's, highlighted the importance of the "human capital" and its improvement through education. This is a concept that I've always made naturally mine. He and his colleagues Mincer and Becker have developed those theories that were already insights of Smith, considering education and training at the same level of the investment as physical

73

capital. If we are talking about investment, therefore, the decisions on human capital must be taken by appropriate expediency, valuing immediate costs and higher income that the investment can make possible throughout their working life. Not at a specific time, but throughout their lifetime! A theory that has stimulated great comparisons highlights how talent, training and knowledge may affect the worker's earning power differentiating it from others. So, I go back to reflect on the contract and on the value of each worker. How can we claim to be "framed" in a generic scheme when each of us is unique and unrepeatable? These formulas, which have certainly ensured compliance with the rules, however, have created so much damage. Just think of the low profitability of public employment, certainly not even remotely comparable to the private sector. To the dismissal of unsuitable workers or even incompetent. To the meritocracy as an unattainable goal. To administer a public body is one of the most difficult thing to do due to these systems of cages that reign supreme. I admire the mayors of our cities that constantly have to

74

face, with great difficulty, the reality that the human resources too often are inadequate to the roles and that are stuck to a contract and can not be used in the best way. Workers who could be excellent accountants, accountants that can not bear the numbers and who would rather deal with the urban decor, engineers involved in the legal department and lawyers who deal with urban planning. All in a general discontent that can only be deleterious and that has only one goal: guarantee a salary that no one can doubt. Patterns made of length of service and salary levels. All mechanical. How can you put to use a talent if we do not make flexible this strange world of work in which most of us live waiting for the retirement age? If it ever arrives... It does not make any sense. In public institutions, in addition to everything, also weighs the turnover of directors, appointed by the policy but unsuitable most of the time. Triggering the inevitable problems also related to the lack of a leading management continuity, to inefficiencies that persist in years until it festers. This is in the best of the hypothesis.

In the worst we know that there is insult on top of injury and is called cheating. Would it not be really the case to revolutionize this world of work? What contracts do we want to talk about ? What flexibility do we want to dream of? Which meritocracy can we cheer for? What value can be recognized and, above all, by whom?

## A PLEASANT SURPRISE

There are actions that thirty years ago we would never have thought doing and that today have become  habit and necessity.  For example: check our email.


It's Tuesday, October 27[th.] I log into my mail account as I do every day. Among a myriad of emails in bold to read, I find one from  Luca, one of the talents that I had selected to add value to the company and, as it has happened to the others, was unable to continue working for the company. The executives have not recognized and appreciated his ability and yet, in my opinion, he had the credentials to do well. I had helped him then to find another job. The first click of the day is his. Subject: severance mail. I read. "*Good evening, Domenico, I want to thank you for so many things, but above all, for showing me how much the human factor is still an essential element in the work. The professionalism and knowledge are necessary elements, however, you transmit every day, to the people around you, that a*

*HUMAN BEING is the backbone of the role that we are playing. You have given me the chance to work for you, this has been one of the most important and significant things of my life, I have left with the same spirit in which I entered: with that hunger that I was telling you about and with the eagerness to get things done. Aware of the fact that I had learned a lot, I regret not being able to offer you, during the period spent together, the harvest of what was sown. I know I've done a lot, but obviously not enough. This does not mean to be pessimistic but to know and demand more and more from ourselves. I have done so. I will treasure all your teachings and I will work to be more and more "structured" as you have claimed from day one. Your judgement counts for me and I would like it to become increasingly greater. With love. Luca*

Sometimes it seems that the succession of events has an unseen manipulator (and who knows if that it's not really so...). There is  absolutely perfect timing, quite upsetting. It all happens at the right time. While I'm thinking of the importance of a man in every circumstance, while I speak about human capital and managerial humanism, here comes this e-mail. Nothing more confirmatory... I'm touched. I am a man, father and manager of a team. How could I not be emotional in front of these words? Back come the tears. Bringing back the red eyes of those who still have a heart.

Inside me, meanwhile, I am reinforcing the idea of a company that does not deserve all this dedication. I am detaching myself from what I no longer feel is a family. That sense of belonging that is vital to do better, has disappeared. It's not like cutting an umbilical cord. Worse. It's like becoming suddenly aware of the fact that there is no blood relationship. A feeling that can be proven by babies swapped at birth in the cradle. No bond with the parents who raised them if not for the affection and gratitude for them, feelings that I no longer have for this family that has now rejected me. I just have to prepare for the meeting with the general manager and the personnel manager. At this point I will reluctantly agree with their request and I have only one goal that I never imagined to have in life: maximize my output. These are assessments that are done only when it is acknowledged to be in a conflict and on the other side of the fence.

## "THE ROLE-PLAY"

Everyone has their own point of view and each also have their role. I've always loved chess because it shows that pedestrians also have their importance in the defence of the king or on allowing the checkmate. You play. You win. You lose. In any case you participate! Each in its place. As in life.

Here comes the fateful date of the meeting with the general manager and the personnel manager. Officially they will inform me what I already know: for organizational reasons I will have to leave the company. At this point it's done and I start negotiations. I introduce a multimedia presentation, with some slides about the things I did in these ten long years. A presentation that leaves them incomprehensibly surprised. I then turn to the staff director, a person certainly different from the prototype of those whom I respect. I express my disappointment at the fact that in a long time, although I was responsible for a team of 20

81

colleagues, I had never had the possibility of a confrontation with him. One thing that is unbelievable for me. Everybody froze, probably because they weren't expecting my presentation and the serenity with which I criticised the executive's work. The role play has now become more complex. Indeed, I don't feel like playing. A few days ago, I heard the news that my friend Lorenzo is no longer a part of the future business plans... I expected it but the confirmation made me ruthless and now, Lorenzo and I have decided to treat this company in the same way: nothing more and nothing less than a number. They treat us as pedestrians but we will have a kings exit!

## HAPPY BIRTHDAY DADDY

There is nothing more beautiful than to dedicate a "victory" to someone who is no longer here and that you would really want by your side. Someone you know for sure that would rejoice with you and for you.

I meet Mariolina, as we agreed, in Milan at 9:00 o'clock. She confirmed the resumption in the mythic company where I had left my heart, and that my father liked so much. This is all I could ask for. I'm happy and this is enough for me. We say goodbye with the smile of who respects each other and with the certainty of an imminent future of serenity. I return to the office to sign the release agreement. From the 1$^{st}$ of January, I will not be in the company that my father never loved. My thoughts go to him. It is inevitable. Today is November 5$^{th}$, the day of his birth, and the "case" wants me to celebrate it with a gift that he would have greatly appreciated. Greetings Dad!

## COINCIDENCES

Have I already said that life seems a tangle of coincidences that are actually miracles? I repeat it again. This is what it is.

Having signed the agreement to leave on the date, "by chance", of my father's birth, always the "case" is that of today, November the 10th, the anniversary of my mother's death. I find myself in my old company to sign a new employment contract. It's midday and I'm cutting the tape with a new goal knowing that in a few hours I will cut another equally important. My daughter will be presenting her thesis this afternoon. Two wonderful things in one day, not the same as many years ago when I lost my mother. Maybe today someone wants to compensate the pain with joy. Mom, you're not a coincidence! I feel you closer than ever! On this anniversary, you're here with me and with my family. You took me by hand and you have accompanied me all these years. I'm still a child and I still feel like a son.

85

## How to dismember a body

Have you  played football, played in a band or  been a part of a rescue or medical team or whatever involves collaboration?   Only then you can really understand what it means to lose a piece or more pieces. When you have  a body and you have to give away the limbs, you have difficulties recognizing the body itself. This is my nature, as I already wrote: I love sharing. Between a soloist and an orchestra, I prefer the orchestra and I've always compared it to life: each of us is an instrument. Everyone can play it, respecting what it is. To recognize the innate and hidden talent in us should be the main concern of every individual. Only in this way you avoid the false notes in the incredible orchestra of life. Each instrument, even what may seem trivial and with a subtle sound, in fact makes a unique and harmonic melody. This success is the result of preparation, sacrifice, continuous exercise and especially love. Everything we do, must be motivated by a feeling: the irreplaceable fuel of our complicated "Super cars"...

This is what differentiates us from machines. We are men. A reflection that stubbornly returns with all his determination.

It's really time to alert my team and only those who are used to working as a team can understand what it feels like. Seated in front of each other, in a meeting convened specifically this November 16th, the air gets chilly when I start to talk with an almost unheard tone. I can not describe this moment. There are no words. So I stop. After the farewell meeting between tears, disappointments and emotion, we decide to console ourselves with a good dinner. We are less than 38 people, including the three guys who do not belong to the team but that I helped to find another job. All aware that the on-going change is not caused by my decision. They all partake in my joy for the new job and are happy at how I handled the situation. Did I run it? Or did someone run it for me? I think back to the series of "cases" that seem not to be so and I smile.

## PEBBLES IN THE SHOES

I do not like revenge. It does not belong to me. Yet this time I have a need that I had not known before: to remove the pebbles from my shoes. It is not a trivial saying, rather very eloquent and needs no explanation.

It's November 17th. I go to the office with a copy of the new contract in the left pocket of my jacket. Near my heart. This is not by chance. Within the various offices I ask for a moment of attention. I wait for the people arriving from various departments and with my inseparable smile I say: "Dear Colleagues, from January 1st, I am back to work where I was ten years ago...". I don't give the news in a negative way. I don't even tell them that the company has invited me to leave and in thirty-six hours I have already found a new job but that is what they already imagine. Then it was the sales manager, the personnel director and the general manager's turn. In all three cases, I introduce myself without the usual formalities and I say: "I have good

89

news! I found a new job!". When people ask me where, I do not hesitate a moment to put my hand in the pocket near my heart. I show them the signed contract: "I'll be back to work here". There are expressions of disbelief and surprise. My new company is a multinational company of prestige and they know it. The pebbles are slipping very slowly out of my shoe but the noise they make is deafening. In a moment it resurfaces to my mind a chat of a few days earlier with the staff director who had literally "spat" a judgment against me. A ruling that was not in heaven nor on earth: he told me that maybe I was not integrated in the company. Me? I had become "famous" for the good relationships I had with everyone! Me, the one who after the goodbye meeting, had the pleasure of having dinner with thirty-eight colleagues sat at my table! Me, that I had lived that dinner through tears and emotions! What does the personnel manager know of all these things and of the other dinners with over fifty colleagues? Of the email received from Luca thanking me for what I had taught him?! Who knows??? If there is a non-integrated one, that's him, because he knows nothing of all this. Now, once I had removed the pebbles from my shoes there remains the ordeal shared with my friend Lorenzo. The attempt to also quickly find an opportunity for him remains an opportunity that we just have to wait for, the same as for the other colleagues who have suffered the same fate.

# THOSE STRANGE INEXPLICABLE CHOICES

In a good story worthy of respect, there is always an "antagonist"...

During my dramatic moments, I've had the chance to have many wonderful colleagues by my side. But not everyone has had the same feeling. One, in particular, was concerned only to ask about the "handing over" without a hint of humanity. I should have expected it but I was hoping that he would have behaved differently. It's my positivity that not everyone deserves. Relying on my well-known patience, I replied, with an "aplomb" that still surprises me, that the "handing over" of the platform created by me, I would spend a maximum of an hour (only because my professionalism and seriousness were suggesting me to do it). There are things that we feel we shouldn't do, not because of pride but because we recognize them to be a waste of time. With him it would be like this. The antagonist has done everything to avoid the contact with the people of my team, of

93

whom, I was still in charge until my final exit. It was clear that he could not wait for me to leave but did not understand that his way of being was isolating him from the others. In fact, he had never been invited to any farewell dinners. For me, these are other pebbles that come out of my shoes. If I think how important the human element is in the workplace and that the sales manager will assign him to what remains of my team, I cringe. Those strange inexplicable choices.

## VALUES THAT ALWAYS REWARD

To tell my story was only right for me, for my family, for my colleagues and for those who live in the same business reality (and I know that they are many). Many guys come to look for me. They are without a job. Together, we look at the resumes and we send them to my acquaintances. When they are called for the interview or for a new job, its a great joy for them and for me!

I believe in values and in being professional. Always. On December 29$^{th}$, the date of my birthday, two days before the final departure from the "tragedy" that is now just a memory, I was in the office, ready for the meeting via Skype with the European head of sales and other officials. I presented the project of "Marketing & Sales" that I had developed. I also received the compliments and, today, I wonder: "would somebody else have done this in my place, and after all what had happened?". It remains an unanswered question because this is me and my way of being has rewarded me. It allowed me to find alternatives in a short time. It allowed me not to give up and to hold on to the positive in spite of everything. To have irreplaceable friends, a wonderful family and two parents closer than ever! I will live more my home, with my wife and this is priceless! I got to know myself better, I got to talk to myself, making myself company, blaming and praising me, hating and loving me. I realized that doing something good for someone makes you feel good too. As I've always done and as I will always do. This experience, that I would never have thought living, has had, however, something good about it.

It caused pain. A lot. Anxieties, tears, sadness but also joy. After all, I should know that before you come to life there are the labor pains. Being a man, I too often forget. I can think of all the sayings that I have repeated as banal expressions or phrases of circumstance. Instead, I realize more than ever how much they represent life itself. I am living proof of the fact that after the storm there is a rainbow, and that there is nothing so bad that it is good for nothing.

 I'm living proof that when one door closes another even better will open, and above all (I want to say in a loud voice to those who feel like their life has ended) the fall is not important. What's important  is the desire to get up. The sayings of our grandparents, our parents are the simple reality! A different reality for everyone, a reality that makes us unique and unrepeatable, offering us constant opportunities to be ourselves, feeling strong and intense emotions. Without them, our lives would be too "poor". And I'm not talking of numbers.

## That feeling we call "friendship"

My friend Lorenzo has always lived my hopes, illusions, gratifications, anxieties and satisfactions. He lived this path with me. At last, came the good news of a new job for him. A great joy for me. But I leave him the burden to tell it.

*When Domenico called me, two things struck me: what he was saying and the grace with which he said it. In a few seconds I realized that he was not joking and it was immediately clear that this news would affect me too. We were too similar: a parallel professional story, the same holding of provenance, the same large account management skills. Domenico is famous for the calmness with which he responds to emergencies. He manages to aloof and analyse all aspects in an emergency situation so as to find an immediate solution. With this same grace he phoned me. It was mid-October. He tried to calm me down, inviting me to stay calm, to think that nothing was going to happen to me.*

99

*That maybe I was even going to get a promotion that would free me from a manager that we both didn't like and didn't appreciate, considering him not suitable for the role. But after a few days my turn arrived. I was informed that from the January 1^{st}, my professional function would no longer be expected and therefore we would have to find an economic agreement to jointly resolve the employment relationship. As the two leaders spoke, I thought of the life expectancy of my children with a fifty-two year old father without a job and with low possibility of relocation. I kept thinking about a life full of difficulties. They uttered a series of empty phrases, with no content, no prospect and no consideration of my personal suffering. I went through some terrible days. The relationship between Domenico and me, the most appropriate word is "friendship", was strengthened. It was clear that we had been the subject of an injustice. The only variable in the game was our salary, higher than that of the other colleagues and the multinational was evaluating only that variable, without wanting to consider the contribution of expertise that we brought and we could continue to bring. Thus, Domenico and I, we both concentrated on how to present the best individual resolution agreement of employment. We reached a agreement very much closer to our requests than the starting point of the company. This allowed me a certain "calmness" for some time. Meanwhile Domenico had made a real magic of immediate professional relocation. A myth! Thanks to God and the talent he gave me, the situation has improved from February. The professional quality and friendships established in all the years of work have allowed me to have a number of interesting opportunities. I found myself in the rare position, rare I would say at my age, to be able to choose from three qualified jobs. No one can imagine, but I understood very well, the level of Domenico's happiness when I called him to inform him that I had just signed a new contract starting from June 1^st^. His call was the second phone call I made after the call to my wife. He might not forgive me for this...*

## EPILOGUE

Domenico's story and of his hypothetical colleagues, is an account of this era. Historical courses and resorts have accompanied us so far. History, a repetition par excellence. It's our root and our Infinite. An example and an experimentation. History that recurs. And today? What are we? Futurists or Romantics?

There is a call for a new humanism. More than a reminder, it is a necessity. A human being has an inestimable value that cannot be overshadowed, ever.

We need to return to consider a man and his dignity as have the authors of history. If it is true that a man has a position, in some ways privileged compared to nature, then he should have more respect than technology and numbers that, therefore, depend on him! A lot has been said about the human capital in the last decades, in economy treaties and in study centres but hardly in the society and in companies! Yet it is so obvious: the production capacity of goods and services depends on the combination of the resources you have available.

The resources are, yes, physical capital, and so are the durable material goods but the resources are also human capital with all the knowledge, education, information, experiences, techniques and creative skills. They are all "means of production". It isn't a sensational discovery and neither is the fact that the physical capital is the result of a human labor. That technology is nothing more than human knowledge applied to production and that the role of education is a fundamental requirement for a good working capacity. Yet, often, all that, remains in the books, in the conference brochures, in some auditorium and some times it becomes business reality (thanks to enlightened entrepreneurs) while everything remains crushed by the arrogance of administrators and entrepreneurs who refuse to change. Many who have been successful so far think they can continue on this path. They are not grateful to an economic situation that enriches no matter what, and at the expense of the future that has now become the present with all the difficulties that we know. Those who have had economic and financial success, too often, are full of pride thinking that they are good and don't have to change anything about what they've done. But nature and history teach us that change is inevitable. If Darwin pointed out that not the strongest nor the most intelligent species will survive, but the one that best adapts to changes, what better time now to show this ability? The economy needs it because it's society that requires it in the first place. If it is true that we have enhanced the technology expecting great things from it, it is equally true that we underestimated a man at the same time, sometimes almost denigrating him. Today, however, it must be admitted that a human being is the centre and is at the centre of what he creates and puts to the service of humanity. The measurement of results is an essential element in any action, even more in the enterprise, and the result is different when the phone is answered by a person rather than a tape. It is different when a person responds to an email rather than a programmed software. It is different when a budget relates it to a person rather than just being a conglomeration of well-analysed numbers with no soul or motivation. And all the above results still vary with the changing of the person responsible for the different roles. So here it's the change. Return to give a value to what is most precious in the company: a human being and not his piece of personal data that still remains a number! The Treccani encyclopedia defines human capital as a: "Set of skills, competencies, knowledge, professional and relational skills typically held by the individual, acquired not only through formal education, but also through a long learning or work experience on-site and therefore not easily replaceable because inherently drawn to the subject that has acquired. Although they can not be measured uniquely, the human capital components, however, determine the quality of the service delivered by the holder, contributing to increase the productivity of an enterprise and to qualify it, influencing the results."

A precise definition, more than exhaustive.

# CONTENTS

www.ingramcontent.com/pod-product-compliance
Lightning Source LLC
Chambersburg PA
CBHW071410170626
46811CB00003B/1333